D0191891

Puffin Books

The Lenski Kids and Dracula

The Lenski kids have a terrible reputation. They are the wildest, naughtiest kids in the neighbourhood. Their mild-mannered parents don't know what to do with them – babysitters come and go, never to return again. That is, until Kim Kip moves in next door.

Noel, Samantha and Craig can't understand why Kim doesn't seem to mind their wicked games and booby-traps. She doesn't even turn a hair when she has an unexpected dip in the pool with her clothes on.

But little do those horrible Lenski kids realise just what's in store for *them* the next time their parents are out . . .

THE LENSKI KIDS
AND DRACULA

LIBBY HATHORN

Illustrated by Peter Viska

Puffin Books

PUFFIN BOOKS

Published by the Penguin Group
Penguin Books Ltd, 27 Wrights Lane, London W8 5TZ, England
Penguin Books USA Inc., 375 Hudson Street, New York, New York 10014, USA
Penguin Books Australia Ltd, Ringwood, Victoria, Australia
Penguin Books Canada Ltd, 10 Alcorn Avenue, Toronto, Ontario, Canada M4V 3B2
Penguin Books (NZ) Ltd, 182–190 Wairau Road, Auckland 10, New Zealand

Penguin Books Ltd, Registered Offices: Harmondsworth, Middlesex, England

First published by Penguin Books Australia 1992
First published in Great Britain by Puffin Books 1993
1 3 5 7 9 10 8 6 4 2

Printed in England by Clays Ltd, St Ives plc
Typsset in 16/18 Bembo

National Library of Australia
Cataloguing-in-Publication data:
Hathorn, Libby.
The Lenski kids and Dracula.
ISBN 0 14 034973 1.
I. Viska, Peter. II. Title.

A823.3

For Dorothy and Louie
L.H.

Chapter 1

They were the wildest, meanest, screamiest kids you ever saw. The whole lot of them. Actually, there were only three, but it felt like a whole lot more – a herd of kids.

There was Noel with the red hair that stood up in spikes all over his head. He had freckles and a wide mouth that turned down at the edges mostly, especially when he yelled, which was often. He was ten and top dog.

There was Samantha with browny-red hair, straight as sticks, and a fringe that covered her eyebrows. She was as tall as Noel and nearly as tough even though she was only eight.

Little Craig had pink hair that fell in beautiful ringlets round his face and down his neck. He looked like an angel but he hardly ever acted like one. He was five and could be downright dangerous.

Oh, and there was Fury too, their dog, a great curly-headed mutt. He was playful and friendly but when the going got rough Fury had several secret places and could hide from the Lenski kids for hours on end. Fury was an extremely clever dog.

Talk about noise! There were blood-curdling whoops and ear-piercing screams and elongated cries (but never, ever whispers) when the Lenski kids were round. And talk about fights! There were kicks, punches, spits and scratches and arm-bending wrestles (and never saying sorry) when the Lenski kids were round. They were wild all right. The wildest!

The funny thing was that their parents were the nicest people ever. You wouldn't believe how nice Mr and Mrs Lenski were. Not wild at all. Polite, sweet and utterly adoring of their three awful kids. Mr and Mrs Lenski looked alarmingly alike. Both were round and pale with dreamy eyes and nervous smiles.

'Kids will be kids,' Mr Lenski would say when neighbours complained yet again

about broken windows, or bikes or legs or something or other the Lenski kids had done. 'Unfortunately,' he always added, a little sadly and with an apologetic smile. 'I'll have to speak to Noel/Samantha/Craig about your son/daughter's broken arm/toy/bike,' he'd say in such a worried way.

3

'Oh, dear,' Mrs Lenski would say in sympathy when some kid on the block showed her a bruise or a scratch or a black eye that a Lenski kid had delivered. 'How awful for you. And you say Noel/Samantha/Craig did that to you? Whatever for? You poor little child. They mean well but they do get a little obstreperous at times, I'm afraid . . . You'll just have to learn to keep right out of their way.'

You had to feel sorry for the Lenski parents all right. They had a lot to put up with.

The Lenski house was in a quiet street. It was a big old place with an upstairs and rambly verandahs and it had a big unruly garden. As you got closer to the front door you realised it was a bit like a bomb-site. Mess everywhere and stacks of it. Mr and Mrs Lenski had wisely decided not to worry about tidying up until the children had grown up. What was the use? they asked one another. And, of course, they were quite right.

There was a tangle of toys, bikes, roller-blades and games from one end of the place to the other. *Broken* toys, bikes, roller-blades and games, naturally. And the kids' bedrooms, if you could get into them (not that you'd want to), were indescribable. But the Lenski backyard was the most interesting place of all. It was very tricky because the Lenski kids had rigged up trap-doors and other booby-traps and all manner of torture for anyone silly enough to go out there.

In the middle of the yard was the delight of their lives. A large swimming-pool in which the Lenski kids spent just about all summer swimming, floating, diving, sailing, rafting, rowing, rotating, sprinting, splashing and crashing and anything else you can do in or on water. They had even rigged up a flying-fox from one end of the yard to the other so they could do 'bombs' into the swimming-pool, creating huge waves that wet the yard and flowed down the booby-traps.

'Aren't they ingenious?' Mr Lenski would say admiringly to Mrs Lenski, inside the cover of the house as one body after another hurtled across the backyard. 'They really plunge into things!'

'Nice to see them getting such fun from simple things on such a hot day,' Mrs Lenski murmured, before turning back to her fifth cup of tea.

'I wouldn't mind a swim, you know, dear,' Mr Lenski said, looking longingly at the blue water.

'Oh, I shouldn't go out there,' Mrs Lenski replied sensibly, looking at the trail of

wreckage that led to the pool, 'not *out there*, dear.'

'I guess you're right,' he said. 'What with the booby-traps and the science experiments. Leave them to it, eh?'

'Absolutely,' she agreed.

And they both went into the lounge room and put on a Beethoven sonata and read poetry out loud to one another to drown out the high-spirited screams coming from the backyard.

Meanwhile, out at the pool, the three played their favourite game of the afternoon. Well, Noel's favourite game. He lay back on a float with an air-cushion under his head. 'I am Count Dracula,' he told them, 'feed me or else' and Craig would sprint across the pool to find the secret store of sweets to feed Count Dracula, as Samantha pushed him up and down the pool, kicking furiously. 'Faster slave,' Count Dracula would order. And sometimes, if it was late and Craig and Samantha had had enough, he'd find himself shoved off the float and all alone in the pool.

'Hey, come back,' Noel would demand.

'Indoor games now,' Samantha would say from the safety of the back door.

'Yeah,' Craig would call as his mother approached with a big, fluffy towel.

'Pikers,' Noel would say, swimming around alone. But not for long. He'd be indoors within five minutes, you could count on it. And they'd be into the next game of hide-your-father's-shoe or make-an-explosive-milkshake or some such thing.

Mr and Mrs Lenski loved their kids to pieces but even *they* got a bit fed up with them sometimes. What with the noise and the activity and the tricks – Noel once put super-glue on his father's chair to see if he would stick to it, and guess what, he did! Not to mention the squeals and screams and fights – Samantha once hit Craig and Noel on the head with the same weapon at the same time just to see if she could get two in one blow and she did! 'A broomstick could probably get

seven in one blow,' she'd said, but Mrs Lenski had confiscated the broomstick. So what with all that and more to put up with in an ordinary day, their parents, much as they loved their kids, sometimes got a bit fed up.

Every so often one of them would say in a quivering voice, after a fresh disaster, 'Enough. I've had enough! We're going out tonight *without* the children.' And the other would always agree, of course, knowing you can push a parent only so far. And absence, even a short absence, can make the heart grow fonder. (And just as well.)

But then there would be the sticky problem of finding a babysitter. The Lenskis were somehow always surprised how hard it was to get a babysitter for their three kids. Babysitters came and babysitters went, never to return again.

'It's usually after the children show them the swimming-pool that they leave,' Mr Lenski would say, in a puzzled voice.

'You're right,' she'd agree. 'I've no idea why they all want to go out there in the first place,' and shivered a little at the thought of it. Yes, babysitters came and babysitters went in rapid succession at the Lenski house.

Sometimes, if a new babysitter could not

be found, they'd have to think in reverse about getting some peace and quiet. They'd send the kids to the movies with their grandparents instead of going themselves, just so that they could have a calm and peaceful evening together, reading poetry about tranquil, calm and beautiful places. But even though both grandparents were a little deaf, they couldn't take too much of the children's chatter on the way to and from the movies.

'We don't mind seeing them from time to time,' they said, kissing the children goodbye with great relief, 'but don't call us – we'll call you . . .' Naturally enough they didn't call very often.

Chapter 2

Then Kim Kip came to live next door. She introduced herself to Mr and Mrs Lenski straight away and said that she'd heard the children in the backyard. She was a lean, athletic-looking girl with short hair and a big generous smile.

You'd have to be deaf not to, Mrs Lenski thought, but, being polite, she didn't say it.

And Kim Kip said she was at acting school, saving up for a motor bike (a Harley-Davidson like her boyfriend's) and she was looking for babysitting jobs, and that she'd be really pleased any time to babysit the Lenski kids.

I've heard that before, Mr Lenski thought, but of course he was too polite to say that, too. (So many babysitters had come and gone. They'd *all* gone in fact, never to return.)

'Well, we'll call on you for sure,' the
Lenskis promised and it wasn't too long
before they did. It was after a particularly
rowdy and disastrous Saturday at home that
they felt the utmost urgent need for a few
hours away from their beloved offspring.

Noel had decided they should all learn
abseiling from the upstairs window. Craig
had got stuck on the bathroom window-sill
and had to be rescued with a ladder by his

14

mother. Samantha decided the upstairs window was not high enough and had climbed up on the roof. 'It's great up here,' she'd called, but then looking down to the yard had decided it wasn't so great. 'Help! Help!' she'd shrieked. So Mrs Lenski had to stage another rescue, this time with the extension ladder. Noel, in the meantime, bored with abseiling, was working out circus tricks in the lounge room.

'You bash the drum, Craigo,' he'd said, 'and I'll ride this wild pony.' He went round and round the lounge room on Fury's back until the dog set up such a yowl Mr Lenski came to rescue him.

'We're going out tonight,' Mrs Lenski said when she met her husband in the hallway where he was still calming a quivering Fury.

'Good idea,' he said, 'but what about a babysitter?' To their surprise Kim Kip was available and willing.

'Now, children,' Mrs Lenski said, as she sat watching them playing with their dinner. Noel was accurately flicking his peas, one by one, into his mashed potato; Samantha was expertly spearing sliced carrot and dumping it in Craig's mouth; and Craig was churning his bread into a round, hard, doughy ball in one hand, ready to throw it when he stopped coughing.

'Kim Kip is coming in from next door to look after you tonight. Be good for her, won't you? Daddy and I won't be too late.' The kids all stopped and stared at their parents. 'Did you hear me?' she asked.

'Hee-haw,' said Noel.

'Oink, oink,' said Samantha.

'Baa, baa,' said Craig.

They'd been playing animal farm not long before.

'Such imaginations!' Mrs Lenski said to her husband, as they got ready to go to the movies to see *In a Monastery Garden*, their particular favourite.

'I know they can be trying, dear, but they are really so bright and they have such wonderful imaginations . . . it never ceases to amaze me. They're playing farms, you know.'

'I can see,' Mr Lenski said, skirting the barbed-wire fence that had been strung up in the living room to form a pigpen. 'Good to see them so caught up in things.' Mr Lenski had developed what could be

called a grim humour about his children.

Kim Kip was standing on the doorstep when they opened the door.

'Oh, yes,' Mr Lenski said, 'I'd forgotten. The babysitter, of course.'

'You've brought books to read?' Mrs Lenski said, wonderingly.

'Well, I thought I might read to the children and then after they go to bed I'll do a bit of reading myself. They're only little so they probably go to bed early.'

They don't go to bed, Mrs Lenski thought, if there's a babysitter. Never ever, but she was too polite to say so.

'You kids do what the babysitter tells you to do. Okay?' Mr Lenski said, suddenly in a hurry to go. 'Oh, by the way, this is Kim Kip from next door – your new babysitter. Say hello,' and he went out the front door.

'Hee-haw,' said Noel.

'Oink, oink,' said Samantha.

'Baa, baa,' said Craig.

'They're playing farms,' Mrs Lenski explained as she went down the path. 'Oh, and there's food in the fridge – at least there was last time I looked. Help yourself.'

Chapter 3

Noel, Samantha and Craig stared at Kim Kip.

'Hi, kids,' she said brightly. 'Want to hear a story or something?'

'Hee-haw,' said Noel.

'Oink, oink,' said Samantha.

'Baa, baa,' said Craig.

'Well, you go right on with your game, then,' she told them, 'if that's what you guys want to do – and afterwards maybe you might like a story.'

'Hee-haw,' said Noel.

'Yeah, I got the message before,' she said and then Kim Kip disappeared into the kitchen.

It was lucky she did that early because there was a plate of cheese and biscuits on the bench that certainly wouldn't have been there for too much longer. Samantha was playing pig troughs and that meant she took all the food she could find and mixed it with water and put it in an empty plant pot. Even Fury, who ate practically anything, didn't want to sample this horrible mess of raw eggs, tomato sauce, cottage cheese, baked beans, salami, hummus, broccoli, lettuce leaves and special vitamin-enriched dog biscuits. The dog slunk off to hide behind the lounge as soon as he could get away.

Kim Kip took her plain biscuits, and a piece of smelly Gorgonzola cheese she was particularly fond of, into the lounge room where the kids, who'd finished their farm game for the moment, were watching television. Noel smiled at the others and then he said sweetly, 'Hey, Kip, you wanna see our swimming-pool?'

'Not just now,' Kim Kip said. 'I was going to read you a story. This really funny story about a cabbage patch.'

'I'd like a story,' Craig said.

But Noel hit him and said, 'Baaaaa.'

'Okay, maybe later,' Kim Kip said, settling on the lounge to read her own book.

Then Noel turned off the TV and pushed an exercise book into her hands. 'Read from this page,' he commanded. 'It's a great bedtime story. We love it!'

'If you want . . .' Kim Kip agreed, trying to make sense of the spider-like writing scrawled all over the page. So the Lenski kids gathered around Kim Kip for their story and she began to read:

So the amazingly big werewolf with the hairy face
and the drooling fangs leapt out of the darkness
and in through the window with teeth bared and
tongue dripping and with blood oozing from
cruel claws.

It killed the rather stupid babysitter with one
chunky bite into her scraggy neck. ~~Althogh~~
~~Althuogh~~ Although it took ages for her to
pass out as he slurped up her blood
like mad.

 And then it went looking for the three
~~innocent~~ innocent little children tucked
up in their beds fast asleep, and grunted
~~horribaly~~ horribly as it sank its mean nasty
bloody ~~teeth~~ into the plump little arms...

 But this wasn't all it did. Oh ~~no~~ no! You
see it was a werewolf freak with a very
vivid imagination and it did something so
terrible you really might not ~~beleve~~
believe it. It....

'Eeerk,' Kim Kip said, pulling a face as she read ahead for a bit and then, 'Yuk, yuk, yuk,' and then, looking up, 'Hmm . . . who wrote this stuff?' she asked.

'It's Noel's story. Isn't it great?' Samantha said. 'He's going to be a writer and do horror stories for movies and things when he grows up.'

'He doesn't really have to wait till he grows up,' Kim Kip said. 'It's horrible enough now.' Noel was pleased to see Kim Kip shrink in horror at his story.

'Go on,' he urged her.

Then Craig said, 'I don't think I want to hear about a werewolf freak. I'd like the cabbage patch story.'

'Actually, I wouldn't mind the cabbage patch story either . . .' Samantha agreed, looking at the dark outside the window.

But Noel hit them both on the head a few times with the exercise book he'd grabbed from Kim Kip's hands, and they said, 'It's a good story, Noel, okay, and the cabbage patch story sucks . . .'

Kim Kip thought it was time to take control, so she said, 'I think you guys'd better go to bed now. You can all read your own books for a while and then lights out, okay.'

Chapter 4

But when the Lenski kids went upstairs, Kim Kip could hear giggles and thumps and she called out to them, 'Hey, you'd better get ready for bed. It's nine o'clock already. I'll be up in five minutes so get in your PJs and clean your teeth and everything.'

With that the house was suddenly plunged into darkness. 'What the – ' Kim Kip exclaimed, jumping to her feet. 'Are you okay?' she called out to them but there was an eerie silence.

She managed to find her way to the stairs, but halfway up she tripped and felt a kind of tangle of something that felt suspiciously like fishing-line around her ankles. Not only that, but where her hands had groped wildly on the stairs there was warm, sticky, oozy stuff all over them.

She wondered for a minute whether she

was bleeding to death, but then smelt the distinct sweetish odour of honey. There were giggles and hiccups and screams from upstairs. Samantha appeared with a torch and helped Kim Kip to her feet.

'Are you okay?' she asked. 'You see, we were playing beehives here. Bees.'

'Bzzzz, bzzzzz,' Noel and Craig sympathised.

It couldn't be their fault she'd tripped in the dark, Kim Kip thought, looking at the three little faces by torchlight, or could it?

'Better check the fuse-box upstairs,'

Noel said to the others. 'What do you reckon?'

'I'll check it,' Kim Kip told them. She didn't want them doing anything dangerous. So she checked, and found the power

had been turned off. She turned the power on again and then said, 'Off to bed now, you lot, and no more games. Okay?'

But Craig took her sticky hand and said,
'We want to show you the pool, we really
do . . .' He seemed so sweet with his big
brown eyes and his pinky golden curls that
she agreed.

'Okay,' she said. He led her out into the
floodlit yard, pointing out the bottomless

pit, the broken plank and the suspended bucket of water.

'You'd better watch out for more of these booby-traps. There's one here and, oh, one here and, that's it, one here, too.'

'Why the booby-traps?' she asked, stepping neatly around them.

'We don't like strangers in our pool,' Samantha explained.

'Yeah, you have to be invited,' Noel added.

'We want *you* to see our pool,' Craig said.

'Up close,' Noel urged. 'It's a really cool pool.'

And he took Kim's other hand as they moved through the stripy slashes of dark and light towards it.

'Cool pool,' Craig echoed, tugging her through the litter of junk that finally led to the tiled edge.

'Yeah, yeah, yeah,' Samantha chanted, coming up close behind Kim Kip and urging her onwards, just a little faster, with a push and a shove.

'I have the strangest feeling . . .' Kim Kip began.

They all said, 'Far out!' and 'Golly gee!'
and they didn't know *how* it had happened
at all. Kim Kip teetered at the edge on the
slippery tiles and then she fell head first into
the swimming-pool, fully clothed, of course.

'Oh dear, you've fallen in the pool,'
Craig said, sounding just like his mother.

'Are you okay?' Noel called, because
Kim Kip had disappeared into the
water, but she hadn't come up
coughing and spluttering as
planned. In fact she hadn't
come up at all.

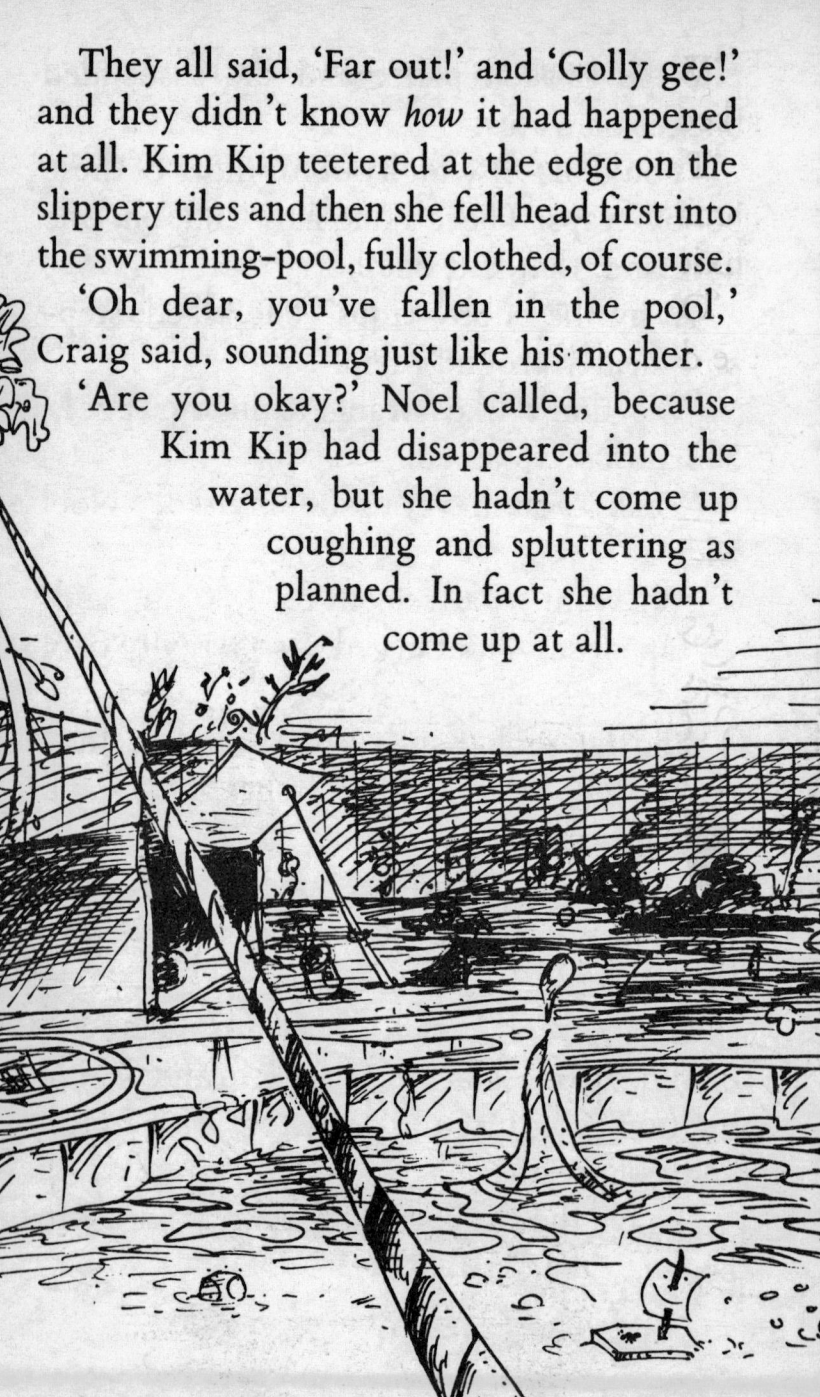

'Well, where's she gone, then?' Craig asked.

'This could be an underwater record,' Samantha said, but she sounded just a bit anxious.

'Or worse,' Noel said, staring hard into the dark depths of the pool.

Then at the far end of the pool, Kim Kip came up, not coughing and spluttering at all, but gliding slowly and gracefully. She lay on her back and did some lazy strokes across the pool.

'It's lovely in the water right now,' she called out to them, 'except for all these clothes I'm wearing. I'm just so glad you took me around all those booby-traps so that you could show me the lovely, lovely pool.' She sounded really happy and really relaxed.

They looked at each other. This wasn't what they'd planned at all for Kim Kip their new babysitter. No, not at all!

Then Kim Kip threw a shoe onto the edge, followed by another.

'What are you doing?' Noel called out, and then a pair of jeans flew through the air.

'Oh, no,' Samantha said. 'Looks like our babysitter's stripping off.'

'Is she swimming starkers?' Craig asked. 'Is she?'

'Looks that way,' Noel said, as Kim Kip's shirt made a neat arc and landed soggily at his feet.

'This is more like it,' Kim Kip called, swimming up and down in their pool in her undies. 'More like a swimming costume, that is.'

'She's not starkers – she's kept her top and her knickers on,' Craig said.

And there she was in her T-shirt and her knickers, doing fancy strokes and underwater plunges and floating dreamily for all of five minutes, really enjoying their pool in her undies and all.

They all took a step back as she climbed out, but she simply shook her jet-black hair and said, 'That was absolutely lovely. Thank you for showing me your wonderful pool, kids.'

'I don't get it,' Craig whispered, but the others didn't answer. 'How come she's not angry at all? How come?'

They were all unusually quiet as Kim Kip put her wet clothes back on and they walked behind her quietly, too, as she cleverly avoided all the booby-traps and squelched into the house. She threw herself down on the lounge and picked up her book. Little streams of water were running out of her

shoes and great stains of water were all over the lounge by now.

'Are you going to sit in your wet clothes, then?' Noel asked, because even Noel knew what happened if you sat about in wet clothes.

'Achoo,' Kim Kip answered.

'You'll catch cold,' Craig told her.

'Achoo,' Kim Kip answered.

'She already has,' Samantha told them.

'Well, I guess we'll go to bed, then,' Noel said, because he didn't know what else to say to their dripping-wet babysitter. He really didn't.

'Yeah,' the others agreed, 'we'd better go to bed,' and then, 'Goodnight,' they said.

'Achoo,' Kim Kip answered, and they all went up the stairs.

Chapter 5

When Mr and Mrs Lenski came home they were still humming the tune from the movie and they seemed braced to take any bad news. But there was none. They were a little surprised to find Kim Kip still steaming by their electric heater.

'I took a dip in the pool,' she explained. 'I do hope you don't mind.'

'You went for a swim?' Mr Lenski said. 'Fully clothed? How odd.'

'She's a very strange babysitter,' he told his wife as they climbed into bed.

'Probably perfect for our children,' Mrs Lenski murmured.

'If she'll ever come again, that is,' Mr Lenski sighed, as he drifted off to sleep.

But she did come again. About a week later when Mr Lenski phoned Kim Kip, she said

she was studying hard for her part in a play and that a quiet night at the Lenskis'd be perfect for her.

'Do you think she's quite right in the head?' he asked his wife. 'A quiet night *here*?'

'She probably enjoys their childish games,' Mrs Lenski said warmly. She felt very cheered at the thought of a whole evening *away* from their childish games.

'Kim Kip is coming to look after you, children,' she told them. 'Do encourage her to borrow swimmers if she wants to go in the pool.'

'Can we go swimming with Kim Kip?' Noel asked.

'If Kim Kip thinks that's a good idea – of course you can.' Mrs Lenski rarely said no to anything her children asked.

'And what are we playing tonight?' Kim Kip asked, when Mr and Mrs Lenski hurriedly left by the front door. She stared straight into their faces.

There was something in the way she spoke that made Samantha feel funny. Something in her tone that made Samantha shiver just a little bit. She didn't know why.

But Noel and Craig didn't notice anything in Kim Kip's tone and said, 'Mum said we could go swimming, but we have to wear swimmers.'

'Oh, we're playing going swimming, are we?' Kim Kip asked.

'No,' Noel explained patiently, 'we're *going* swimming, okay?'

'Okay by me,' Kim Kip agreed, striding through the house. She remembered where every single booby-trap was and reached the edge of the pool uninjured. Even Noel was impressed.

Then she pulled off her T-shirt and her jeans and Noel and Craig and Samantha looked the other way. But this time she had a pair of swimmers on underneath. Kim Kip made a perfect dive into the pool.

'Well, what are you waiting for?' she asked them and she disappeared underwater.

They ran inside for their swimmers and when they came out they couldn't see Kim Kip anywhere.

'She's probably improving her underwater record,' Samantha said as she dived in. The Lenski kids were great swimmers and they loved playing make-believe-on-water, so they got right into their games. They didn't notice the figure on the flying-fox at the other end of the yard – poised, ready.

Noel lounged on the float, not Count Dracula this time, but telling the others, 'I am King Noel the Great – so push me, me hearties!' They did for a while but Craig eventually got fed up and pushed his brother right off. Then he and Samantha played Loch Ness monster games, diving and surfacing in a flurry of white waves and making unbelievably horrible noises across the water, while Noel showed off his backstroke back and forth across the pool.

'Who's afraid of the Big Bad Monster?' sang little Craig. 'No, no, no, not I!'

But it was Craig who screamed loudest because there was suddenly something fearsome dangling right above him. Not a Loch Ness monster but one even more frightening. A dark figure with red eyes and a dripping wet tongue and weird sharp teeth and the face of a wolf was hovering right there, right over them. Craig swam for the edge as fast as he could.

'Do you see what I see?' Noel suddenly yelled, but the others had already leapt out of the pool. 'It's – well – it's exactly like – gulp . . .'

'*Dracula!*' Samantha screamed in real terror, and then, 'Mum, Dad, Kim Kip, anybody!'

'It's him,' Craig choked.

'No way,' Noel said, trying to laugh as he climbed out of the pool too. 'It's just pretend . . .'

'Mum, Dad, Kim Kip,' little Craig called out too, looking around helplessly.

The Dracula-like figure jumped expertly off the flying-fox and spoke in a gravelly, hot voice. 'I've been told about you guys,' he said. 'That you like doing mean things. Izzat right?' He was at least two metres away but his black shiny arms were reaching towards them and his furious mouth was twisting most horribly as he took a long step.

'Only sometimes,' Noel answered, because he wanted to show the others he wasn't scared of this weird-looking thing that had flown right out over their pool. Not too scared, anyway.

'And messy, dirty things. Izzat right?'

'Just a bit,' Craig said, because he was dead scared and he hid behind Samantha, shaking with fright.

'And you 'specially like hurting people. Izzat right?'

'Only little hurts,' Samantha said. Maybe this Dracula is pretend, she was thinking, and then again maybe he is for real. And if he was for real then she knew she should watch every word she said.

'So I reckon you should come with me. I know a place where the weirdest and the meanest and the dirtiest people hang out. It's great and you three kids'd just love it. I've come to take you because we need some mean, dirty, rotten kids like you, we really do. There are plenty of pushers and shovers and punchers and kickers so you'd get on fine. Oh, and it's always semi-dark with lots of bats (bloodsuckers of course) and

cobwebs, so very suitable for terrorising people. Yes, you'd all fit in there perfectly.'

'It's not Dracula. No way,' Noel said, peering into the burning eyes and trying to act tough so they would fade away. 'It's a Dracula look-alike, that's what! I reckon it's – '

But the Dracula look-alike grabbed Noel very firmly by the arm. And the Dracula look-alike lifted him up in the air. When he came face to face with the fangs it didn't look like a Dracula look-alike at all. With its red, glowing eyes and its slobbering mouth and its gleaming white fangs it looked exactly like – well – the real thing.

And the voice. It was the worst sound he'd ever heard, grating and hoarse and yet quite, quite clear. It struck terror into Noel's soul. After all he was a Dracula expert! It was a nightmare come true. It was *Dracula!*

'Come right on. Why hang around here?' Dracula screamed into Noel's face. 'You can do mean, ugly, nasty things all day in the place I'm taking you. And I've heard you're top dog . . .'

'Hey, wait a minute,' Noel said. 'I'm not a dog. And you – can – just – put – me – down.'

When poor little Craig heard mention of the word dog he let out a howl. 'Fu-u-ury,' he called and the old dog hearing his name called so loudly came out of hiding for a moment from behind the tool-shed.

'Here, boy,' Samantha called, catching sight of Fury's pointy snout. 'Save us, Fury! Skitch him, Fury!'

But Dracula let out a blood-curdling howl of his own and Fury took off inside to crawl under Mr and Mrs Lenski's bed and there he stayed put for the entire evening.

Noel, meanwhile, tried very hard to bite and kick this tough, mean Dracula. But Dracula pushed him high into the air on the flying-fox and suspended him over the pool.

'Let me go, you pig!' he shouted. But when Dracula shook him and roared extra

loudly he was thoroughly frightened, and to
Samantha and Craig's surprise he began to
call out pathetically, 'Mum, hey, Mum,
Dad. Heeeelp!'

'Put him down,' Samantha cried.

'Yeah, let go our brother,' Craig
shrieked, too.

'You mean, you guys would like to come with me and leave your poor brother, who can do such mean kicks and punches, behind?'

'No, we don't want to go at all,' they whimpered. 'No way.'

'And what about you, big brother? We need mean nasty little punks like you where I come from.'

'Put me down you . . . . .!' Noel insisted, and you could see he was absolutely terrorized now. His face had gone white and his mouth was quivering. At that moment, Dracula did let go. Dropped him clean into the pool and Noel came up coughing and spluttering, of course.

'Mum – help, Mum,' Craig began, as Dracula moved forward and swooped him up in his arms.

'And you're next. I've heard you're downright dangerous, you are.'

'Not me,' Craig said, punching and pinching and trying to act downright dangerous. But all to no avail because Dracula was so big and so strong that Craig was held at arm's length out over the pool.

'Dad – Kim Kip – anybody,' Samantha cried, as Craig was dumped in the pool too, and she was gathered up herself by the strong arm of Dracula.

'And you're a great meanie, I've heard. We need you, too.'

'What do you mean, "meanie"?' she asked as he dropped her – kersplash – dangerously close to the terrified Craig.

They thought Dracula would do terrible things to them now that he had the three of them bobbing around the pool up to their necks in water. He would have for sure, because he let out another of his spine-chilling cries followed up by a roar of heart-rendingly awful laughter. But at this moment, to the intense relief of the three children, Kim Kip suddenly appeared out of the dark on the other side of the pool. And, boy, did she look mad! She had some sort of weapon in her hands, too.

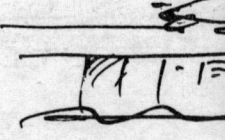

Chapter 6

'That was Dracula,' Craig kept saying over and over again, 'that was Dracula here in our pool. That was Dracula. That was Dracula . . . *Dracula!*'

'I thought it was you dressed up first,' Noel told Kim Kip, as he sat by the edge of the pool rubbing his bruised arm. 'First of all. Until you showed up, that is.'

'Whatever would make you think such a thing?' Kim Kip said.

'Well, who was it?' Samantha asked, 'I mean, *who was it?*'

'That was Dracula, I tell you,' Craig said and Kim Kip nodded.

'I reckon,' she agreed. Noel and Samantha looked anxiously at each other.

'I reckon,' Samantha whispered and Noel nodded, 'Me, too.'

'Well,' Kim Kip said thoughtfully, 'he shouldn't come back . . .'

Inside when they were dry and sitting in their pyjamas by the electric heater, Kim Kip said, 'I'll read you some of *your* Dracula story if you like, Noel.'

But Noel shivered and said, 'Nup. Not my Dracula story tonight.'

'Are you sure?'

'Sure I'm sure, meathead,' he said angrily, and then remembering Dracula's last words he added, 'What I mean is – er, no thanks, Kim Kip. No thanks a lot!'

'Had enough of Dracula for one night?' Kim Kip asked.

'You could say that,' Noel said.

'She just did,' Craig added, 'she just said – '

'Here's your stinky cheese and biscuits,' Samantha said sweetly, bringing Kim Kip some Gorgonzola. This was just as well because Noel was about to hit his little brother over the head.

'Would you read the cabbage patch story?' Craig asked her. Strange to say, Noel didn't say anything more.

And the three of them actually sat there quietly while Kim Kip read them the very funny book about a kid who found a very strange baby in a cabbage patch, and as she read Kim Kip ate her Gorgonzola cheese biscuit by biscuit.

'Hey, that'd be great cheese to take to school,' Noel said finally. 'It's so stinky and we could play a really good trick with it. We could put it in that new little kid's desk . . .' But Kim Kip was staring at him in such a funny way that he said, 'Well, maybe not, I guess. Maybe not a trick with that stinky cheese with the new kid . . . maybe with the teacher or something . . .' His voice trailed off.

When Mr and Mrs Lenski came home they were surprised to see the lounge room almost tidy and to hear that the children had brushed their teeth and gone to bed.

'I'm not saying we didn't have a little game first,' Kim Kip said. 'We were in the swimming-pool for quite a while.'

'Oh, how nice,' Mrs Lenski said. 'It's lovely you can play with the children like that. I hope the booby-traps didn't bother you too much. Such high-spirited little things. Their idea of fun, you know . . .'

'Not at all,' Kim Kip replied.

'She's just like a kid herself,' Mr Lenski said, when Kim Kip had gone home.

'As long as she wants to go on babysitting our kids, Humboldt,' said Mrs Lenski, 'I really don't care how much of a kid she is. Isn't it strange, though – such a gentle person and yet she seems to have a really good effect on our little darlings. I can't think why . . .'

Mr Lenski didn't bother answering Mrs Lenski – well, he couldn't really, because he didn't want to think why and anyway he'd fallen fast asleep.

But Mrs Lenski was quite right. Kim Kip did have a good effect on the Lenski kids. Of course they didn't stop being awful altogether and Noel did think there was something quite familiar about the voice of Kim Kip's boyfriend when they first met him on his motor bike outside Kim Kip's house, especially when he said 'Izzat right' a few times. (But Noel didn't like to comment because Kim Kip's boyfriend, Morrie, certainly didn't have fangs dripping with blood or a particularly hairy face or anything.) And after all he had a way of staring at Noel that made him think it would be nice to be his *friend*! Morrie was big and tall with a gravelly voice and he told them he did weight-lifting *and* kick-boxing as well as his acting!

No, the Lenski kids didn't become goody-two-shoes overnight. They were still pretty awful. They were still noisy and wild and loud and rude and screamy but somehow after Kim Kip and Dracula in the pool, they didn't seem to be quite so mean and vicious any more.

There were fewer broken arms and

noses and windows in the street where they lived. And there were sometimes whole stretches of quiet in the Lenski household when there were no rowdy games and no fights going on at all. At first Mr and Mrs Lenski thought they were in the wrong house.

'Do you think our Noel is quite well?' Mr Lenski asked Mrs Lenski one day. 'He actually tidied up his room this morning.'

'I think he's just growing up at last,' Mrs Lenski sighed.

'He said Kim Kip's boyfriend Morrie is going to help him build a model boat and he said you need room to do it properly.'

'And after that he's teaching them all kick-boxing,' Mrs Lenski added.

'How nice,' Mr Lenski murmured.

'And Samantha has invited us to swim in the pool,' Mrs Lenski went on, 'this afternoon.'

'Well, I don't want to go too far,' Mr Lenski said. 'I mean it's pretty dangerous out there in the yard, dear.'

'But Samantha said she and Craig and Noel have taken down all the booby-traps and defused the baby bomb in the tool-shed and everything.'

'Why?' he asked suspiciously.

'So that we can swim there if we want to. And others.'

'Others?'

'Kim Kip's boyfriend Morrie is coming over.'

'I like this Kim Kip's boyfriend – whoever he is,' Mr Lenski said, going to find his antique swimmers.

'Morrie's got a part in the new play,' Kim

Kip told the Lenski kids as she sat by the pool with Fury at her feet, 'and you'll never guess who he's playing.'

But Noel had already slipped into the water and was swimming away. He had some Condy's Crystals in his hand, a dye that would turn the entire pool, and the people in it, a purple colour when released at the other end.

And Craig was diving under, and Samantha had just worked out a way of doing a star jump that set up huge waves across the pool – so maybe they didn't hear Kim Kip say, 'Morrie's playing Count Dracula. Don't you think he'd do it well?' because they didn't answer. Not one of them.